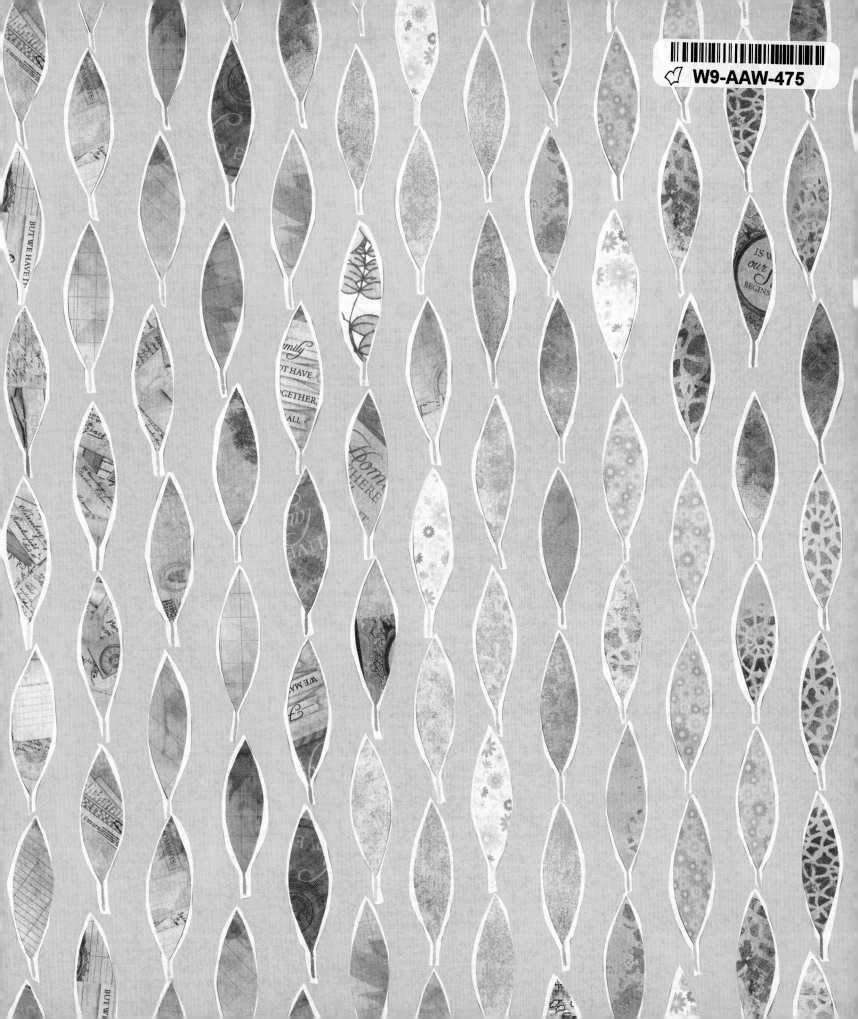

No Ordinary Jacket

Sue-Ellen Pashley

illustrated by

Thea Baker

CANDLEWICK PRESS

The jacket was no ordinary jacket.

It was soft, like dandelion fluff.

It was warm, like the afternoon sun.

It was comforting, like a hug

from your favorite teddy bear.

And it had four dazzling buttons

down the front.

The jacket went home with Amelia.

She wore it everywhere.

She wore it to preschool.

And to Auntie Kath's house.

And to the park.

And to bed.

Until, one day, she couldn't
fit into it anymore.
So Mom suggested she give
it to her little sister, Lilly.

Lilly wore it everywhere.

She wore it to the park.

And to Nana's house.

And to the library.

And even to the beach.

Until, one day, she couldn't
fit into it anymore either.

So Lilly put the jacket

on her favorite doll.

Lilly and her doll had tea together.

And played in the sandbox.

And jumped on the trampoline.

Until Lilly grew big

and went to school . . .

and stopped playing with her doll.

The jacket didn't seem so special anymore.

It was still soft and warm and comforting,

but now it had paint on the elbow.

And dirt on the hem.

And threads coming loose at the collar.

And only three dazzling buttons down the front.

The jacket was left in the corner of Lilly's room,

half hidden under the wardrobe.

No longer going to the park.

Or to Nana's house.

Or to preschool. Or to bed.

Until one day, Cornflake the cat had kittens.

They all curled up on the jacket.

They were five of the softest, warmest,

most beautiful things that Lilly had ever seen.

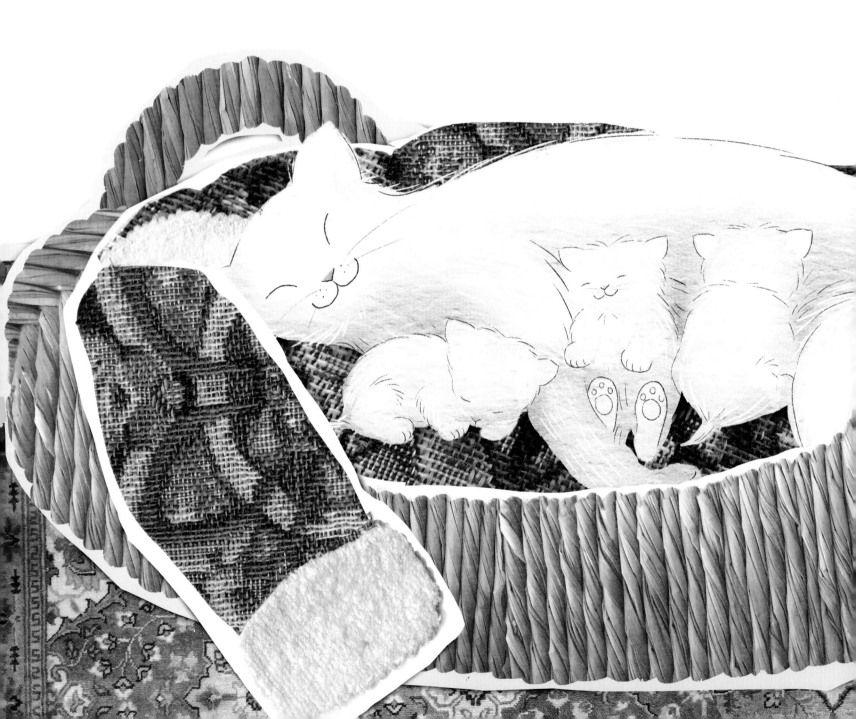

She tucked the jacket around them, and it held them and kept them warm. And when the kittens were bigger, they went to their new homes.

Mom picked up the jacket.

She looked at its painted elbow.

And its dirty hem.

And its thread-pulled collar.

And the cat fur that covered it.
And said, "We should get rid
of this dirty old thing."

Lilly was sad.

Was her jacket a dirty old thing?

Even with its two remaining

dazzling buttons?

She thought of when she'd

worn it to the beach.

And Nana's house.

And the park.

And to bed.

And how it had held the kittens.

Mom was very clever.

She measured and cut and sewed

until . . .

the teddy bear was

no ordinary bear.

It was soft, like dandelion fluff.

It was warm, like the afternoon sun.

It was comforting,

like wearing your favorite jacket.

And it had two dazzling buttons

down its front.

For Jack, Gabby, and Lawson —
who dream and imagine in so many
different ways — and are happy
to let me dream and imagine.
Love you with all my heart, always.

S. P.

For Zuri,
no ordinary girl;
love you more than
a thousand stars.

T. B.

First U.S. edition 2020
First published by Walker Books Australia 2019

Library of Congress Catalog Card Number pending
ISBN 978-1-5362-0966-2

CCP 25 24 23 22 21 20
10 9 8 7 6 5 4 3 2 1

Printed in Shenzhen, Guangdong, China

This book was typeset in Cochin.
The illustrations were done in mixed media.

The illustrator wishes to thank and acknowledge Kaisercraft Pty
Ltd for use of their craft papers in her collage illustrations.

Candlewick Press
99 Dover Street
Somerville, Massachusetts 02144

visit us at www.candlewick.com

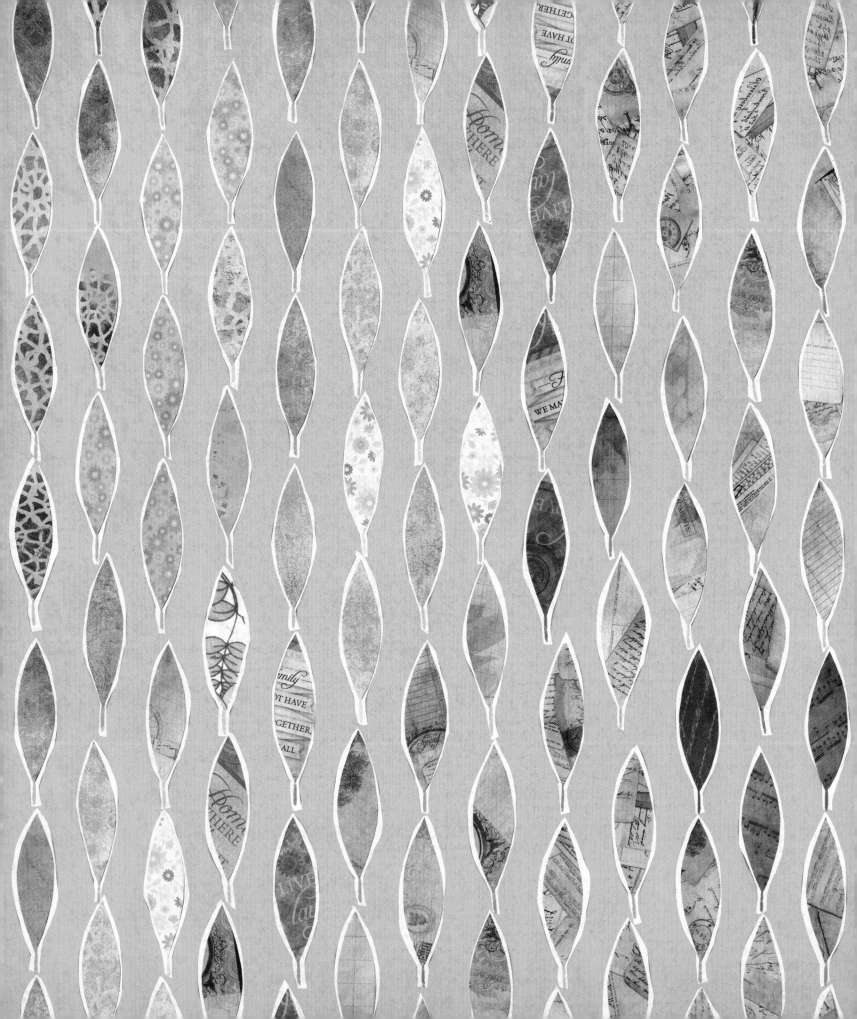